A MAGIC CIRCLE BOOK

the king, the dragon, and the witch

by **JEROME R. CORSI**   illustrated by **SYLVIE SELIG**

THEODORE CLYMER
SENIOR AUTHOR, READING 360

GINN AND COMPANY
A XEROX COMPANY

the king,
the dragon,
and the witch

Once upon a time,
    for that's how all tales must begin,
there lived a king
    who really didn't like being a king,
and a dragon
    who really didn't like being a dragon,
and a witch
    who liked nothing better than being a witch.

5

The King was a good king.
In fact everyone agreed
they had never seen a better king.
He was fair and just and
very kind to the people.
He never sent anyone
to the dungeon without feeling
a little sorry that he had to.

6

The King did not like

> to tax the people,

> or give everyone orders,

> or do the things a king always does.

He liked to walk in the forest,

> and go fishing,

> and talk to the villagers

> without being called "Your Highness."

The Dragon was an old dragon.

> In fact everyone was surprised

> that one dragon

> had lived so long.

> He could not roar

> or breathe fire anymore,

> or even frighten pretty maidens

> who passed his way.

The Dragon liked to walk through the woods,
and wade in a cool river,
and sometimes play with small children.

But the Witch was wicked.
In fact everyone agreed
they had never seen a more wicked witch.
She lived in a cave far away
where few people ever saw her.
Everyone liked it that way.
Even the Witch liked it that way
because she didn't like people —
especially happy people.
She would stay up late at night
to think of terrible things
to do to people.
She would cast a spell
whenever she could —
sometimes for no reason at all.

The King liked the Dragon.

They often walked together

through the forest

and talked things over.

The King liked to talk to the Dragon.

He listened well.

Besides,

there were no other dragons left

in the whole kingdom.

Some had been killed by knights.

Others had grown old and died.

Others had moved away.

Sooner or later

all the dragons but

one

had died or been killed.

But the Witch didn't like
the Dragon at all.
She remembered the days
when there were lots and
lots of dragons —
dragons who breathed fire
and killed people.
She remembered when
people were more afraid
of dragons than witches
and she didn't like that at all.
(Witches like to be feared more than anyone.)
The Dragon was old and kind now,
but he was still a dragon,
and that was enough
to make the Witch hate him.

One day when the King
　　was walking through the forest
　　(it was fall now and he liked
　　to hear the leaves crunch under his feet),
　　he came upon the Witch.
"You're making too much noise," she shouted.
"You don't really mind the noise,"
　　said the King.
　　"What you don't like is that
　　walking through the forest
　　and hearing the leaves crunch
　　under my feet makes me happy."
This really made the Witch angry
　　because witches
　　don't want people to be happy.

"Now you've got me so mad
    I'm going to cast a spell on you,"
the Witch told the King
with a gleam in her eye,
for this was her chance
to be really wicked.
(That's the only time witches are happy.)

The Witch got ready to cast her spell.
    She ran around and around
    jumping up and down,
    first on her right foot
    then on her left.
    She waved her hands in the air
    around and around
    until she was tired.
Then she took a deep breath and
    pointed at the King.

14

One, two, three,

I cast a spell on thee.
I'll make you say
you wish this day
you hadn't walked by me.
Every day when the clock chimes four
a trouble I'll send your way.
Then I'll stay up all night to think of more
to bring you the following day."
Suddenly
the Witch had a thought.
Here was a way
to get rid of the Dragon!
So she added,

16

"There's only one way
for you to be free
of the wicked spell
I cast on thee.
Listen carefully and
you shall see.
"A wicked beast roams the forest.
He's a terrible sight to behold.
You must drive him away
forever to stay
or more bad luck I'll unfold."
The King started to walk back
to the castle.
He could still hear
the leaves crunch
under his feet
as he walked along,
but he was no longer happy.

17

He knew what the Witch meant.
　　She wanted him
　　to get rid of the Dragon.
But the King couldn't do that
　　because the Dragon was his friend.
　　And the King couldn't send
　　his friend away —
　　not even to break a spell.
The King waited to see
　　what would happen.
　　The next day
　　he was sitting on the throne
　　waiting for four o'clock.
　　At exactly four o'clock,
　　his throne fell apart
　　and the King was left sitting
　　on the floor.

18

Another day
   he was walking across the bridge
   leading from the castle.
   At exactly four o'clock,
   the bridge broke
   and the King was left sitting
   in the moat.

For weeks the spell went on.
    One day
    the King was reading in the library.
    At exactly four o'clock,
    all the books slipped off the shelves.
    The King was left sitting
    on the floor
    with books all around him.

The King didn't know what to do.
He couldn't drive away
the Dragon,
but he couldn't go on and on
with something terrible happening
to him every day.
He thought and thought
about what the Witch had said.
The Dragon roamed the forest
and he was a beast,
but he wasn't a terrible sight
to behold.
In fact the King had come
to think of the Dragon
as not a dragon at all,
but as a friend.
And friends
certainly aren't wicked.

The King decided that

    there was only one thing he could do —

    he had to see his friend, the Dragon.

    But he waited until after four o'clock

    so that nothing would happen

    while he and the Dragon talked.

The King told the Dragon

    about the spell

    that the Witch had put on him.

    He told the Dragon

    that he didn't want

    to get rid of him

    because they were friends.

    And the King

    couldn't send his friend away,

    not even to break the spell.

    But what other beast roamed the forest

    and was a terrible sight to behold?

The King and the Dragon
    sat thinking a long time.
    Suddenly the King said to the Dragon,
    "I know — I know
    who I must get rid of!
    Certainly the Witch
    is a terrible sight to behold.
    And she does live
    in the forest
    and she certainly
    acts more like a beast than you,
    my friend.
    I must drive the Witch away
    never to come back
    if I am to be free of the spell."
The King and the Dragon formed a plan.
    They waited until very late at night
    when the Witch was asleep.

Then they crawled
ever so quietly up to the cave
where the Witch lived.
They stepped on the leaves,
but they were very careful
to step softly and slowly
so that the leaves wouldn't crunch.

The Dragon hadn't breathed fire for years.

But now he really tried.

He breathed in very, very hard,

thought the meanest thought he could,

and breathed out a flame

which he never thought he had.

When he breathed out the fire,

the Dragon also let out a roar.

(It wasn't much of a roar because the Dragon

was old and hadn't roared in a long time —

but just the same it was a roar.)

Suddenly the Witch woke up.
   She looked outside her cave and
   saw the Dragon
   breathing fire and roaring.
   She was so frightened
   that she jumped out of bed and
   ran and ran and ran.
   Some people say
   she never stopped running.

28

The King and the Dragon
were both sure she
would never come back.

At four o'clock the next day,

the King and the Dragon

went for a walk.

Nothing happened.

In fact the sun was shining.

The King had frightened away

the only beast

who roamed the forest

and was a terrible sight

to behold.

The spell was lifted.

The King and the Dragon were very, very happy.

For once

the King didn't mind

being a king,

the Dragon

was very glad he was a dragon,